THE DEVIL'S MASK

KENZIE SKYE

One

The bell above the shop door chimes, its delicate tinkle a stark contrast to the oppressive silence that hangs over Grandmother's antique store. I inhale deeply, the scent of aged wood and musty fabric filling my lungs as I shrug off my red coat. The worn crimson wool slips through my fingers like water, a comforting weight as I hang it carefully on the brass hook by the door.

"Lily, dear, is that you?" Grandmother's voice floats from the back room, papery thin and quavering.

"Yes, Gran," I call back, my eyes sweeping over the dimly lit shop. Dust motes dance in the weak sunlight filtering through grimy windows, casting long shadows across the hodgepodge of curiosities that line every available surface. "I'm here for my shift."

As I move deeper into the store, the floorboards creak beneath my feet, each step echoing in the cavernous space. The air grows thicker, heavier, as if the very atmosphere is saturated with the whispers of a thousand forgotten stories.

My gaze drifts to the forest visible through the front window, its dense foliage a writhing mass of green and shadow. A shiver runs down my spine, unbidden, and I wrap my arms around myself. Why does it feel like the woods are watching me?

"There's a new shipment in the back," Grandmother says, emerging from behind a towering bookcase. Her silver hair catches the light, forming a halo around her weathered face. "Be a dear and start unpacking, won't you?"

I nod, forcing a smile. "Of course, Gran. Anything interesting this time?"

Her eyes, sharp despite her age, narrow almost imperceptibly. "Nothing you need concern yourself with, child. Just...be careful."

The warning in her tone sends another chill through me, but I push it aside. "I always am," I assure her, making my way to the storeroom.

The back of the shop is even more cluttered than

the front, a labyrinth of stacked boxes and precariously balanced furniture. I pick my way through carefully, my fingers trailing along the rough edges of wooden crates and smooth curves of porcelain vases.

As I reach for the first box of the new shipment, something catches my eye. Half-hidden beneath a threadbare tapestry, a glint of gold winks at me in the dim light. Curiosity piqued, I pull the fabric aside, revealing an ornate mask unlike anything I've ever seen.

My breath catches in my throat as I lift it gently. The mask is heavy, cool against my skin, its surface etched with intricate swirls and symbols I don't recognize. As I turn it over in my hands, a strange warmth begins to spread through my fingertips, up my arms, settling deep in my chest.

I trace the contours of the mask with trembling fingers. The urge to put it on is overwhelming, a siren song I can barely resist.

"Lily!" Grandmother's sharp voice shatters the moment. I whirl around, the mask clutched guiltily to my chest. She stands in the doorway, her face pale, eyes wide with fear. "Put that down. Now."

"I... I'm sorry," I stammer, confused by the intensity of her reaction. "I was just—"

"That mask is not for you," she says, her voice

low and urgent. She crosses the room in quick strides, snatching the mask from my hands. "Some things are better left alone, child. Especially those that belong to the Devil in the forest."

"The Devil?" I repeat, my mind reeling. "Gran, what are you talking about?"

But she's already turning away, the mask disappearing into the folds of her shawl. "Forget you ever saw it, Lily. For your own sake." She pauses at the door, her shoulders sagging. "And whatever you do, don't go into the woods alone."

As she leaves, I'm left standing in the dim storeroom, my hands still tingling from the touch of the mask, my heart racing with questions I'm not sure I want answered. Outside, the forest looms closer than ever, its secrets calling to me with a voice I can no longer ignore.

Gran told me to stay out of the forest.

But I've never been very good at doing what I'm told.

———

The wicker basket digs into my arm as I trudge deeper into the forest, my red coat a vibrant slash against the muted greens and browns. Grandmother's warning echoes in my mind, but the pull of the woods is stronger than ever. The trees loom overhead, their branches reaching out like gnarled fingers, casting dappled shadows across my path.

A twig snaps behind me, and I whirl around, heart pounding. That's when I see him.

He emerges from the shadows like a specter, tall and imposing. But it's the mask that captures my attention—a wolf's visage, carved with exquisite detail, its empty eyes seeming to pierce right through me. I take an involuntary step back, my breath catching in my throat.

"You shouldn't be here," he says, his voice low and gravelly. Despite the mask, I can feel the intensity of his gaze.

I straighten my spine, willing my voice not to shake. "I'm delivering supplies to my grandmother's cottage. Who are you to tell me where I should or shouldn't be?"

He takes a step closer, and I'm hit with a mix of fear and...something else. Something that makes my pulse quicken in a way that has nothing to do with fright.

"I am Vail," he says, "and these woods are not safe for someone like you."

I arch an eyebrow, curiosity warring with caution. "Someone like me?"

Vail's hand twitches, as if he wants to reach out but thinks better of it. "Someone innocent. Untouched by the darkness that dwells here."

His words send a shiver down my spine, but I can't tell if it's from fear or excitement. Part of me wants to run, but a larger part is inexplicably drawn to this mysterious, masked stranger.

"What darkness?" I ask, taking a small step towards him. "What's really going on in these woods?"

Vail's shoulders tense. "Forces beyond your understanding. Creatures that hunger for the light in souls like yours." He pauses, and I can almost feel the weight of his gaze through the mask. "You must not venture here after nightfall. That's when they hunt."

I should be skeptical. I should laugh off his warnings as the ramblings of a madman or an elaborate prank. But there's an undercurrent of truth in his words that resonates with something deep inside me.

"Why should I believe you?" I challenge, even as part of me already does.

Vail takes another step closer, close enough now that I can see the intricate carvings on his mask, smell the scent of pine and something wilder clinging to him.

"Because," he says softly, "I've seen what lurks in the shadows. And I couldn't bear to see it claim you, Lily."

My name on his lips sends a jolt through me. "How do you know my name?"

But Vail is already backing away, melting into the forest shadows. "Go to your grandmother's. Deliver your supplies. But heed my warning, Lily. When darkness falls, make sure you're far from these woods."

As he disappears, I'm left standing alone on the path, my heart racing, my mind swirling with questions. The rational part of me wants to dismiss his warnings, but something deeper, more instinctual, tells me that Vail speaks the truth. And as I continue on my way, I can't shake the feeling that my life has just irrevocably changed.

———

I bolt upright in bed, my heart pounding, sweat beading on my forehead. The dream clings to me like cobwebs, refusing to dissipate even as consciousness takes hold. I can still feel the weight of the mask on my face, see the looming shadow before me.

Closing my eyes, I try to steady my breathing. "It was just a dream," I whisper to myself, but the words ring hollow.

The mask from Grandmother's shop. In my dream, I wore it, its ancient contours molding to my face as if it had been crafted for me alone. And before me...I shudder, remembering the towering figure shrouded in darkness, radiating power and something else. Something that called to me.

I throw off my covers, padding to the window. The forest looms beyond, a sea of shadows under the pale moonlight. It seems to pulse with life, with secrets. With possibility.

"What's happening to me?" I murmur, pressing my palm against the cool glass. The forest has always been there, always been a part of my life, but never like this. Never so...enticing.

I think of Vail's warning, his intense gaze behind that wolf mask. "Stay out of the woods after dark," he'd said. But standing here now, the night forest calls to me like a siren's song.

My red coat hangs by the door, a splash of color in the dim room. I reach for it, my fingers tracing the familiar fabric. "Mom," I whisper, "what would you do?"

But there's no answer, just the quiet of the night and the persistent pull of the forest. I slip the coat on, its weight comforting and somehow empowering.

"This is crazy," I tell myself, even as I move towards the door. "Downright foolish."

Yet I can't resist. The dream, the mask, Vail's warnings—they all swirl together, creating a mystery I'm compelled to unravel. As I step outside, the cool night air caresses my skin, and the forest seems to breathe a sigh of welcome.

I take a tentative step towards the treeline, then another. But then I stop and bite my lip, considering, before I change direction.

I need answers.

Two

The bell above the shop door jingles as I step inside, my heart pounding with anticipation. Dust motes dance in the dim light filtering through grimy windows, and the familiar scent of old books and polished wood fills my nostrils. But something's off. The air feels heavy, charged with an unseen energy that makes the hair on my arms stand on end.

"Grandma?" I call out, my voice echoing in the eerie silence. No answer.

A shiver crawls down my spine.

I move deeper into the shop, weaving between crowded shelves and display cases. My fingers brush against cool metal and smooth glass, searching for any sign of disturbance. That's when I spot it—a yellowed piece of paper on the counter, covered in my grandmother's spidery handwriting.

My breath catches as I read the words:

The Devil's Mask awakens. Ancient curse stirring. Must protect the forest. Find me where the shadows dance.

"What does this mean?" I whisper, a chill running down my spine. The mask I found...could it really be tied to some ancient evil?

I clutch the note, my mind racing. Where would Grandma have gone?

The forest. It has to be the forest.

Without a second thought, I'm out the door and heading for the treeline at the edge of town. The sun is setting, painting the sky in shades of blood and fire. As I plunge into the woods, the temperature drops, and mist curls around my ankles.

"Grandma!" I call out, pushing through dense underbrush. Branches snag at my clothes, leaving tiny scratches on my skin.

Something tugs at the edge of my consciousness —a feeling, an instinct I can't explain. It's as if an invisible thread is pulling me deeper into the forest. I hesitate, torn between logic and this strange compulsion.

"This is crazy," I mutter to myself. "I should go back, call the police..."

But even as the words leave my lips, I know I won't. *Can't*. Whatever's happening, it's tied to my family, to secrets I'm only beginning to uncover. I have to see this through.

I take a deep breath and let that inexplicable feeling guide me. As I walk, the forest seems to shift around me. Shadows deepen, trees loom closer. And then, suddenly, a path appears where moments ago there was only tangled undergrowth.

My heart races as I stare at the narrow trail winding through the trees. It seems to shimmer slightly, as if not quite real.

I clench my fists to stop my hands from shaking.

With one last glance behind me at the familiar world I'm leaving behind, I step onto the hidden path and into the unknown.

As I venture deeper along the hidden path, the air grows thick with an otherworldly presence. The hairs on the back of my neck stand on end, and I can't shake the feeling of being watched. Suddenly, a familiar figure materializes before me, his piercing blue eyes locking onto mine.

I startle. He's not wearing the wolf mask this time.

And damn, is he gorgeous.

My heart skips a beat as I take in his striking features—chiseled jawline, full lips, strong brows. The moonlight filters through the leaves, casting a soft glow on his angular face. Every inch of his face draws me in like a magnet.

"Vail," I breathe, my heart skipping a beat.

He steps closer, his armor glinting in the dappled light. "Lily, you must turn back," he warns, his voice low and urgent. "The mask you found—it's not what you think."

I straighten my spine, meeting his gaze. "What do you know about it?"

Vail's expression darkens. "It's tied to an ancient being known as the Wolf King, who once ruled this forest. The mask is a conduit for his power, his curse."

My mind reels. "The Wolf King?" I vaguely remember hearing something about an old legend involving a wolf king. "But that's just a legend, isn't it?"

"Legends often have roots in truth," Vail says, his

eyes searching mine. "This one is more real—and more dangerous—than you can imagine."

I think of my grandmother's cryptic notes, of the mask's eerie pull. "Is that why my grandmother disappeared? Because of this Wolf King?"

Vail's silence is answer enough. My resolve hardens. "Then I have to keep going. I need to find her."

"Lily, please," Vail implores, reaching out as if to touch me, then pulling back. "You don't understand the forces you're dealing with."

I shake my head, my voice firm despite the tremor in my hands. "I can't turn back now, Vail. I won't."

As I push past him, the forest seems to come alive around me. Shadows dance at the corners of my vision, and the trees themselves appear to shift and warp. The path beneath my feet twists, leading me deeper into the heart of the woods.

A twig snaps nearby, and I whirl around, my breath catching in my throat. In the distance, I catch a glimpse of glowing eyes—not one pair, but several. My pulse quickens as I make out the silhouettes of wolves, their forms shimmering and ethereal.

"This isn't possible," I whisper, even as the wolves draw nearer, their movements fluid and unnatural.

I back away slowly, my mind racing. Are these

the Wolf King's servants? Guardians of the forest? Or something else entirely? The air grows heavy with magic and menace, and I realize with a start that I'm no longer in the world I thought I knew.

As the otherworldly wolves close in, their eyes fixed on me with an unsettling intelligence, I can't help but wonder: have I made a terrible mistake?

A snarl rips through the air, and I stumble backward, my heart pounding against my ribs. The nearest wolf lunges, its spectral form a blur of moonlight and shadow. I brace for impact, but it never comes.

Instead, a dark figure materializes between me and the ethereal pack. Vail stands tall, his imposing form a barrier against the otherworldly threat. With a gesture of his hand and a command in a language I don't understand, the wolves halt their advance.

"Stand down," Vail's voice resonates with power, sending a shiver down my spine. The wolves whimper and retreat, their glowing eyes dimming as they melt back into the forest.

I stare at Vail, my mind reeling. "How did you...? What *are* you?"

He turns to face me, his piercing blue eyes holding centuries of sorrow. "I am what the forest has made me, Lily. Nothing more, nothing less."

The weight of his words settles over me like a shroud. "You can control them. The wolves, they listen to you."

"Control is a strong word," Vail says, his voice low and tinged with regret. "Let's say we have an...understanding."

I take a step closer, drawn by the mystery surrounding him. "Are you connected to the Wolf King? To the mask?"

Vail's expression darkens. "You're asking questions you're not prepared to hear the answers to. The danger you face is far greater than you realize."

"Then help me understand," I plead, frustration building within me. "My grandmother is missing, and I need to find her."

He reaches out, his hand hovering near my face but not quite touching. "Your quest may cost you more than you're willing to pay, Red."

The use of my nickname startles me. "How do you know—?"

"There's much I know," Vail interrupts, his voice softening. "And even more I wish I didn't."

The forest seems to hold its breath around us, the air thick with unspoken truths and hidden dangers. And I can't shake the feeling that I'm standing on the precipice of something vast and terrifying, with Vail as my only lifeline in this strange, magical realm.

Vail's hand grips my upper arm firmly, his touch sending a jolt of electricity through my body despite the layers of clothing between us. "I can't let you go any deeper into the forest, Lily," he says, his voice a low rumble that resonates in my bones. "It's too dangerous."

I open my mouth to protest, but the intensity in his gaze stops me short. There's a power in those blue depths, a command that demands obedience. And beneath that, a flicker of something else—concern, perhaps even fear. For me.

"I'll take you home," Vail says, leaving no room for argument. He turns, his hand still locked around my arm, and begins to guide me back the way I came.

As we walk, the forest seems to shift and change around us. The mist parts like a living curtain, revealing hidden paths and secret glades. Bioluminescent flowers bloom in the shadows, their delicate petals pulsing with an ethereal glow. The air hums with the sound of distant waterfalls and the whispers of creatures I can't quite see.

It's a world of wonders, of magic beyond my wildest dreams. And yet, with Vail's hand on my arm, his presence solid and unyielding beside me, I can't fully embrace the enchantment. My mind is too busy trying to process the man himself—the mystery he embodies, the secrets he carries.

I steal glances at him as we navigate the twisting trails, taking in the strong lines of his profile, the way his dark hair brushes against the collar of his armor. There's a grace to his movements, a coiled power that speaks of centuries of experience. And that dominance, the way he takes control...it stirs something deep within me, a primal response I can't quite suppress.

I shake my head, trying to clear the traitorous thoughts. This is hardly the time or place for such distractions. But as Vail guides me over a fallen log, his hand shifting to the small of my back to steady me, I can't help the shiver that runs down my spine.

We emerge from the forest at the edge of town, the streetlights flickering to life as dusk settles over the quiet streets. Vail walks me to my doorstep, his presence a silent guardian in the gathering shadows.

"Stay out of the forest, Lily," he warns, his voice low and urgent. "Promise me."

I hesitate, torn between the desire to uncover the truth and the instinct to heed his words. "I can't just abandon my grandmother, Vail. I need answers."

His jaw clenches, and for a moment, I think he

might argue. But then he sighs, his shoulders sagging slightly under an invisible weight. "I know. But please, be careful. There are forces at work here that you can't begin to comprehend."

I nod, my throat tight. "I will.

THREE

The door swings open with an ominous creak, revealing a scene of utter chaos. My heart plummets as I take in the devastation before me. Grandmother's cherished antiques lie shattered on the floor, their delicate fragments glinting in the dim light. The acrid scent of something burned lingers in the air, mixing with the musty odor of overturned furniture.

"No," I breathe, stepping gingerly over the threshold. My eyes are drawn to the walls, where bizarre symbols have been scrawled in what looks disturbingly like blood. They pulse with an eerie energy, sending shivers down my spine.

Vail's presence looms behind me, a dark shadow

at my back. His hand hovers near the hilt of his sword as he surveys the wreckage. "We cannot linger here," he murmurs, his voice low and urgent. "It isn't safe."

I turn to face him, searching his piercing blue eyes for answers. "What happened here? Who did this?"

His jaw tightens, a flicker of something—regret? fear?—passing over his stoic features. "The Wolf King's agents. They seek what you possess."

My hand instinctively goes to the pocket where I've stashed the mysterious mask. Its weight seems to grow heavier with each passing moment. "But why? What does it mean?"

Vail's gaze sweeps the room once more before settling on me with an intensity that steals my breath. "I cannot explain here. We must go, now. Do you trust me?"

The question hangs in the air between us, fraught with unspoken tension. Every instinct screams at me to run, to find my grandmother, to make sense of this madness. And yet...there's something in Vail's eyes, a flicker of humanity beneath the cursed knight's facade, that compels me to nod.

"Lead the way," I whisper, my voice barely audible over the pounding of my heart.

Vail's hand closes around mine, surprisingly warm despite his otherworldly aura. He guides me swiftly through the wreckage of my home, pausing only to retrieve a small satchel from a hidden compartment beneath a floorboard. The weight of unanswered questions presses down on me as we slip out the back door and into the gathering twilight.

The forest looms before us, its ancient trees standing sentinel at the edge of town. Vail leads me deeper into its embrace, the shadows growing longer and more oppressive with each step. The familiar sounds of Stormwind fade away, replaced by an eerie stillness that sets my nerves on edge.

"Where are we going?" I ask, my voice sounding small in the vast quiet of the woods.

Vail's grip on my hand tightens fractionally. "To a place hidden from mortal eyes for centuries. A sanctuary...and a battleground."

We come to a stop before an enormous oak, its gnarled trunk easily wider than my arms could encircle. Vail presses his palm against the rough bark, murmuring words in a language that sends tremors through the earth beneath our feet. The tree groans, its roots shifting to reveal a yawning chasm in the forest floor.

"After you," Vail says, a hint of dark humor coloring his tone.

I hesitate at the threshold, peering into the inky blackness below. The scent of damp earth and ancient stone wafts up, carrying whispers of forgotten magic. With a deep breath, I step forward, plunging into a world I never knew existed beneath the streets of Stormwind.

Vail follows close behind, the entrance sealing seamlessly above us. Soft bioluminescent fungi line the walls of the tunnel, casting everything in an ethereal blue glow. The air grows thick with magic, tingling against my skin as we descend deeper into the earth.

"What is this place?" I ask, my voice hushed with awe and trepidation.

"The last bastion of the Old Ones," Vail replies, his words echoing off the stone walls. "Those who remember the time before the Wolf King's reign...and those who have been waiting for your arrival, Lily Rhodes."

My steps falter at his words, a chill running down my spine that has nothing to do with the underground chill. "My arrival? What do you mean?"

Vail's expression is grim as he turns to face me, the ghostly light casting deep shadows across his features. "The Wolf King has returned, awakened from his centuries-long slumber. And your family, Lily...your blood holds the key to either his downfall or his ultimate triumph."

I stare at Vail, my mind reeling. "My family? But we're just...normal people. Antique dealers."

A wry smile tugs at Vail's lips. "Normal people don't typically come into possession of ancient, powerful artifacts."

The mask.

Its weight suddenly feels heavier in my bag. I pull it out, its bone-white surface gleaming in the ethereal light. "You mean this?"

Vail's eyes lock onto the mask, a mixture of reverence and fear in his gaze. "That, Lily, is the key to controlling the Wolf King himself. And you...you are the last of the Red Cloaks."

The words hit me like a physical blow. "Red Cloaks?"

"Warriors," Vail explains, his voice low and intense. "Guardians who once stood against the wolves, protecting the realm from their hunger for power and flesh."

I run my fingers over the mask's smooth surface, feeling an odd warmth emanating from it. "And I'm supposed to... what? Fight the Wolf King?"

Vail's expression darkens. "It's not that simple." He takes a deep breath, seeming to steel himself. "I am...a cursed knight, Lily. Bound to serve the Wolf King until that mask is destroyed."

My eyes widen, and I instinctively take a step back. "You serve him? Then why are you helping me?"

"Because I have no choice," Vail says, his voice laced with centuries of pain. "But I can warn you. If you use that mask, you risk falling under the King's control yourself. The power it offers...it's seductive, dangerous."

I clutch the mask tighter, torn between fascination and fear. "So what am I supposed to do?"

Vail's piercing blue eyes meet mine, filled with an intensity that makes my breath catch. "That, Lily Rhodes, is a choice only you can make. But know this: the fate of our world may very well rest upon it."

———

The mask sits on my nightstand, its empty eyes seeming to follow me as I toss and turn. Sleep eludes me, my mind a whirlpool of conflicting thoughts. Vail's warning echoes in my head, but beneath it, I feel a growing pull—an insistent whisper that grows louder with each passing moment.

I squeeze my eyes shut, willing myself to drift off, but the moment unconsciousness takes hold, I'm plunged into a dream unlike any I've experienced before.

Mist swirls around my ankles, cool and damp. The scent of pine and wild roses fills the air. Before me stands an impossibly tall figure, cloaked in shadow and fur. Golden eyes pierce through the gloom, fixing on me with an intensity that makes my heart race.

"Lily," a voice rumbles, deep and resonant. It feels ancient, powerful. "You bear my mask. You carry the blood of those who would chain me."

I try to speak, but my voice catches in my throat. The figure takes a step closer, and I feel the weight of his presence like a physical force.

"But you are different," he continues. "You understand the allure of power, the thrill of embracing one's true nature."

His words send a shiver down my spine—equal parts fear and...something else. Something I'm afraid to name.

"I don't–" I finally manage to choke out. "I don't want power."

A low chuckle reverberates through the misty forest. "Don't you? Think of all you could accomplish. The wrongs you could right. The protection you could offer to those you love."

Images flash through my mind: my grandmother's ransacked house, the symbols on the walls, the fear in Vail's eyes when he spoke of his curse.

The Wolf King's voice softens, becoming almost tender. "You needn't be afraid, little Red. Together, we could reshape this world. All you need do is embrace your destiny...and set me free."

I jolt awake, heart pounding, sheets tangled around my legs. My hand reaches out, almost of its own accord, fingers brushing against the cool surface of the mask.

I stand and pad over to the door. I push it open and creep down the dark hallway until I come to a room door that's cracked open.

My curiosity gets the better of me and I peek inside.

I creep down the hallway, my bare feet silent against the cold stone floor. A sliver of warm candlelight spills from a door left slightly ajar, beckoning me forward like a moth to flame.

As I draw closer, a soft sound reaches my ears—a rhythmic rustling, punctuated by barely audible gasps and grunts. Curiosity wars with propriety inside me, but as always, my inquisitive nature wins out.

I peek through the crack in the doorway. The scene before me sends a shock of heat straight to my core.

Vail lies sprawled on a simple cot, his sculpted torso bared and gleaming with a sheen of sweat in the flickering light. His head is thrown back, eyes shut tight, dark hair spilling across the pillow. One powerful hand moves beneath the sheet draped over his hips, the fabric shifting with his strokes.

I know I should look away, flee back to the safety of my room, but I'm frozen, transfixed by the raw, primal beauty of him. The cords of his neck strain as a low moan escapes his lips and his movements intensify.

The sheet slips lower and my breath catches. I've never seen a man aroused before. The thick, straining length of him both terrifies and fascinates me. Warmth pools low in my belly as I imagine how he would feel in my hand. In my mouth. Inside me.

Seemingly of their own accord, my fingers drift to the hem of my nightgown, gathering the thin fabric up my thighs. I barely suppress a gasp as I brush my fingers against the slick, sensitive flesh at the apex of my legs.

I've never done this before, and I don't know what force is driving me, just that I'm following some instinct I can't control.

Vail's breath grows harsher and his hand moves faster. I match his rhythm, biting my lip to stay silent. A deep flush stains my cheeks but I'm too far gone to care, too drunk on strange new sensations to stop.

His back arches off the cot and I watch, enraptured, as ecstasy overtakes his face.

"Lily," he groans, spending himself over his fist. My mouth falls open a I watch the thick, white ropes shoot from his body.

Hearing my name on his lips, wrapped in pleasure, is my undoing. I muffle a cry against my palm as my own release crashes over me, knees trembling with the force of it.

Momentarily dazed, I nearly stumble back in my haste to retreat before he discovers me. I scurry down the hall on shaking legs, pulse pounding in my ears.

Back in my room, I lean against the closed door and try to catch my breath. My skin feels too tight, my heartbeat erratic. Unbidden, my gaze falls on the mask, still sitting innocuously on the nightstand.

I recall the Wolf King's words from my dream, silky and seductive. The images from Vail's room dance behind my eyelids, merging with darker, wilder fantasies.

I shake my head, trying to clear it.

I have to remember what's important, and that's saving Gran.

Four

The moonlight casts long shadows across my borrowed room in Vail's hideout. I run my fingers along the edge of an ornate mirror, its silvered surface cool against my skin. My reflection stares back at me, but the girl I see feels like a stranger—red hair glowing like embers, green eyes haunted by newfound knowledge.

"Are you ready to leave?" Vail's low voice breaks the silence, sending a shiver down my spine.

I turn to face him, my breath catching as I take in his imposing figure. Even in the dim light, his piercing blue eyes seem to glow with an otherworldly intensity. My cheeks flush when I remember what I caught him doing last night, remember what *I* did, and I quickly look away, willing those thoughts away.

"I...I think so," I stammer, trying to ignore the way my heart races when he's near. "I still can't believe any of this is real."

Vail's expression softens almost imperceptibly. "The world you knew and the world that truly exists have always been one and the same, Lily. You're simply seeing it with new eyes now."

As he speaks, I notice a fleeting vulnerability in his gaze, gone so quickly I wonder if I imagined it. My fingers itch to reach out and touch him, to bridge the chasm of secrets that lies between us. Instead, I clench my fists at my sides.

"How will we find her?" I ask, my voice barely above a whisper. "My grandmother...she could be anywhere in the magical realm by now."

Vail moves closer, his armor gleaming in the moonlight. The scent of pine and smoke clings to him, reminding me of the forest that has always bordered our town. "I have my ways," he says cryptically. "But the journey will not be easy. Are you certain you're prepared for what lies ahead?"

I swallow hard, trying to quell the fear rising in my chest. The weight of my lineage, of the destiny I never asked for, threatens to crush me. But beneath the terror, a fierce determination takes root. "I have to be," I reply, meeting his gaze steadily. "She's all the family I have left."

Something flickers in Vail's eyes—approval, perhaps, or a shared understanding of loss. He nods once, then turns toward the hideout's entrance. "Then let us be on our way. The night grows short, and we have far to travel."

As we step out into the streets of Stormwind, the city seems to shift and blur around us. Neon signs flicker with arcane symbols, and shadows move in ways they shouldn't. I stick close to Vail, hyper-aware of his presence beside me.

"Stay alert," he murmurs, his hand resting on the hilt of his sword. "There are those who would hinder our quest, and others who may prove valuable allies. Trust nothing at face value."

A cool breeze carries the scent of rain and something wilder—magic, perhaps, or the stirring of ancient powers. I shiver, pulling my cloak tighter around me. "Vail," I begin hesitantly, "why are you helping me? Aren't you bound to serve the Wolf King?"

He doesn't answer immediately, and I wonder if I've overstepped. But then he speaks, his voice heavy with an emotion I can't quite place. "Some bonds run deeper than curses, Lily. Some choices, once made, cannot be unmade. That is all I can say for now."

His words leave me with more questions than answers, but I sense it's all he's willing to share. As we make our way through the shadowy streets, I can't help but wonder what secrets Vail keeps locked away behind those sorrowful eyes. And despite everything, I find myself drawn to him, even as a voice in the back of my mind whispers warnings I can't quite ignore.

———

The silence between us grows thick with unspoken tension. I'm about to press Vail further when he suddenly stops, his posture rigid. "We're being followed," he whispers, his breath warm against my ear.

My heart races as I scan our surroundings. The streets of Stormwind seem deserted, but shadows dance at the edges of my vision. "Where?" I breathe.

Vail's hand finds mine, his touch electric. "This way," he says, pulling me into a narrow alley.

We duck behind a dumpster, the smell of rotting garbage assaulting my senses. Vail's body presses against mine, and I'm acutely aware of every point of contact. His eyes, usually so guarded, meet mine with an intensity that steals my breath.

"Lily," he says, his voice low and urgent. "There's something you need to know about me. About why I'm cursed."

I swallow hard, torn between curiosity and fear. "Tell me," I whisper.

Vail takes a shaky breath. "I was once a knight, sworn to protect the innocent. But I...I betrayed my comrades. For power. For immortality." His eyes close, pain etched across his features. "The Wolf King offered me everything I thought I wanted. I didn't realize the cost until it was too late."

The revelation hits me like a physical blow. I want to recoil, but there's nowhere to go. "You...betrayed them?" I manage to choke out.

"Yes," he says, his voice barely audible. "And I've paid for it every day since. The curse...it's my punishment. My eternal shame."

I search his face, looking for any sign of deception. But all I see is raw, agonizing honesty. Can I trust him? Should I? My mind reels with doubt, even as my heart aches for the torment I see in his eyes.

Before I can respond, a noise from the street makes us both freeze. Vail's hand tightens on mine. "We need to move," he whispers.

We slip out of the alley, keeping to the shadows. As we round a corner, I nearly collide with a hooded figure. I stumble back, but more emerge from the darkness, surrounding us.

"The Red Cloak's descendant," one of them hisses. "We've been waiting for you."

Vail draws his sword, positioning himself between me and the strangers. But to my surprise, they lower their hoods, revealing faces marked with the same birthmark I bear.

"We are your kin," a woman says, her eyes boring into mine. "And we bring a warning. The Wolf King's mask must be destroyed...but the price will be your life, Lily Rhodes."

The world seems to tilt beneath my feet. My life? I look to Vail, but he's glaring at the women, and I hear a low growl rumble in the back of his throat. "Be gone!" he roars at them.

They scamper away, but I stand frozen, my heart pounding against my ribs like a caged bird. The weight of destiny presses down on me, threatening to crush my resolve. My life...the cost of saving everyone else. The words echo in my mind, a haunting refrain.

"No," I whisper, more to myself than anyone else. "I can't...I'm not ready for this."

Vail's piercing blue eyes lock onto mine, a storm

of emotions swirling in their depths. "Lily," he says, his voice low and urgent. "We need to focus on finding your grandmother first. One step at a time."

I nod, grateful for the anchor he provides. "You're right," I say, drawing a shaky breath. "Grandmother needs us. I can't let her suffer because I'm...afraid."

The air between us seems to crackle with unspoken tension. Vail reaches out, his fingers brushing my arm, sending a shiver through me. "Fear doesn't make you weak, Lily. It makes you human."

I lean into his touch, craving the warmth and stability he offers. "And what about you?" I ask, my voice barely above a whisper. "What makes you human, Vail?"

His eyes darken, and for a moment, I see a flicker of vulnerability beneath his stoic exterior. "You do," he murmurs, so softly I almost miss it.

The admission hangs between us, fragile and potent. I feel a surge of warmth in my chest, a connection deepening despite the doubts that still linger.

"We should move," Vail says, breaking the moment. "The Wolf King's minions could be close."

I nod, squaring my shoulders. "Lead the way. I'm ready."

As we slip through the shadowy streets of Stormwind, I can't shake the feeling that with each step, I'm moving closer to a fate I'm not sure I can face. But with Vail by my side, his presence both comforting and electrifying, I find a strength I didn't know I possessed.

The future may be uncertain, fraught with danger and sacrifice, but for now, I cling to this moment, to the connection growing between us. It's a light in the darkness, guiding me forward, one step at a time.

FIVE

The air shimmers before us, a veil of ghostly mist parting to reveal a jagged archway of twisted obsidian. My breath catches in my throat as I reach out, fingertips tingling as they brush the ethereal surface.

Vail's presence looms beside me, a shadow made flesh. His piercing blue eyes meet mine, filled with centuries of sorrow and resolve. "Are you certain you wish to proceed, Lily? Once we cross this threshold, there may be no turning back."

I swallow hard, steeling myself against the tendrils of doubt creeping into my mind. The weight of destiny presses down on my shoulders, but I force my voice to remain steady. "I have to, Vail. For my grandmother. For all of us."

With a nod, he extends his hand. I hesitate for a heartbeat before lacing my fingers through his. His skin is cool to the touch, yet a warmth spreads through me at the contact. Together, we step through the shimmering veil.

The world shifts and blurs around us. When my vision clears, I gasp. We stand in a vast cavern, its walls glistening with an oily sheen that seems to writhe and pulse. Shadows dance at the edges of my perception, taking on monstrous forms before dissipating like smoke.

"Stay close," Vail murmurs, his grip on my hand tightening. "The Wolf King's illusions are powerful. Trust nothing but what you can touch."

As if in response to his words, the air before us ripples. A figure materializes—my grandmother, her face etched with pain and fear. "Lily!" she cries out, reaching toward me with trembling hands. "Help me, please!"

My heart seizes. "Grandma!" I start to move, but Vail's iron grip holds me back.

"It's not real," he says, his voice low and urgent. "Remember, Lily. This is a test."

I squeeze my eyes shut, fighting against the overwhelming urge to run to her. When I open them again, my grandmother's form wavers, revealing glimpses of something dark and twisted beneath.

"You're right," I breathe, forcing myself to look away. "But it feels so real. How can we tell what's genuine in this place?"

Vail's expression softens for a moment, a flicker of the man he once was shining through. "Trust in yourself, Lily. Your heart knows the truth, even when your eyes deceive you."

We press onward, the cavern seeming to stretch endlessly before us. With each step, new horrors manifest. I see friends and loved ones in peril, hear their screams echoing off the walls. But beneath it all, a wrongness pulses, a discord that jars against reality.

"He's trying to break us," I realize aloud, my voice barely above a whisper. "To make us doubt everything, even ourselves."

Vail nods grimly. "The Wolf King feeds on fear and despair. Stay strong, Lily. Remember why we're here."

I take a deep breath, centering myself. The red cloak around my shoulders feels heavier, almost alive. I focus on its warmth, on the legacy it represents.

As we venture deeper into the shadowy realm, I can't shake the feeling that we're being watched. The very air seems to press in around us, thick with ancient magic and malevolent intent. But with Vail by my side, I feel stronger.

Safer.

The air grows thicker, almost suffocating, as we push deeper into the Wolf King's domain. Vail's breathing becomes labored, his steps faltering. I glance at him, worry gnawing at my insides.

"Vail?" I whisper, reaching out to steady him. "What's wrong?"

He shakes his head, jaw clenched. "The curse...it's getting stronger. I can feel it clawing at my mind."

A low growl echoes through the cavern, sending shivers down my spine. Shadows coalesce, taking the form of massive wolves with glowing red eyes. They circle us, teeth bared.

"Stay behind me," Vail orders, drawing his sword. But his hand trembles, and I see conflict raging in his piercing blue eyes.

"You can control them, right?" I ask, fear creeping into my voice.

He doesn't answer, instead lunging at the nearest wolf. His movements are sluggish, lacking their usual grace. The wolf dodges easily, snapping at Vail's exposed arm.

"No!" I cry out, heart pounding. I step forward, not knowing what I can do but unable to stand idle.

Suddenly, warmth spreads through me, emanating from my red cloak. It pulses with an energy I've never felt before, both familiar and alien. Without thinking, I throw my hand out towards the approaching wolves.

A burst of crimson light erupts from my palm, enveloping the creatures. They yelp and retreat, cowering in the shadows.

"Lily..." Vail gasps, staring at me in awe. "How did you...?"

I look down at my hands, still tingling with power. "I...I don't know. It's the cloak, I think."

He nods, a mix of relief and something else—wariness?—in his eyes. "It seems you've awakened your heritage. We may stand a chance after all."

As the words leave his mouth, a chilling howl pierces the air. More wolves emerge from the darkness, their eyes fixed on us with murderous intent.

"Can you do it again?" Vail asks, raising his sword.

I swallow hard, feeling the power thrumming beneath my skin. "I'll try."

As the wolves charge, I reach deep within myself, drawing on the strength of generations past. The cavern fills with crimson light, and I pray it will be enough to keep us both alive.

The crimson light pulses around us, beating back the encroaching shadows. But with each wave, the darkness returns, pressing in with renewed determination. Vail and I fight side by side, our movements synchronized in a deadly dance. His sword flashes, cleaving through the monstrous forms while my newfound power keeps the worst at bay.

Yet even as we push forward, I can feel my strength waning. The cloak's energy thrums through my veins, but it's a wild, untamed thing. Each burst leaves me more drained, my body trembling with the effort of channeling this ancient magic.

Vail senses my struggle. In a moment of respite, he pulls me close, his forehead resting against mine. "You're doing well, Lily. Stay strong. We're almost there."

I nod, drawing comfort from his proximity. The scent of leather and steel clings to him, grounding me in the midst of this nightmare realm.

We press on, the cavern narrowing until the walls seem to close in around us. The air grows thick and oppressive, each breath a struggle. Even the shadows seem to take on weight, clinging to our skin like oily residue.

And then, we reach it. A towering door of blackened wood, etched with sinister runes that seem to writhe and squirm. An aura of malevolence emanates from it, so palpable I can almost taste it on my tongue.

"The Wolf King's lair," Vail murmurs, his voice tight. "Beyond this point, his power will be at its strongest."

I step forward, hand outstretched, but an invisible force repels me. The air crackles with dark energy, sending me staggering back into Vail's arms.

"There's a barrier," I gasp, my skin crawling from the contact. "How do we get through?"

Vail's expression turns grim. His gaze flickers to my bag.

I follow his eyes, realization settling like a leaden weight in my stomach. I open my bag and look inside with a gasp. The mask seems to pulse with a life of its own, its empty sockets boring into me, beckoning.

"No," Vail says, his hand gripping my arm. "Lily, you don't have to do this. We can find another way."

But even as he speaks, I can see the truth in his eyes. There is no other way. The Wolf King's power is too strong, his hold on this realm absolute. Only by donning the mask, by embracing the very darkness we seek to overthrow, can we hope to reach him.

"I have to, Vail." My voice trembles, but I force myself to meet his gaze. "You know it as well as I do."

He closes his eyes, pain etched into every line of his face as he nods with resignation.

I place the mask on my face and instantly feel darkness surround me.

Yet, there's also an incredible sense of power...

And then I start hearing whispers.

Whispers of power.

Wealth.

Anything I desire.

You belong with me, child. We will reign together with you as my queen. You are destined to be mine.

I shake my head and ignore them.

The Wolf King's lair looms before us, a twisted palace of shadow and bone. Each step closer sends a shiver down my spine, the mask on my face growing heavier, more insistent. Its whispers grow louder, promising power, freedom, everything I've ever wanted.

"Lily?" Vail's voice cuts through the haze, concern etched on his face. "Are you alright?"

I blink, realizing I've stopped walking. "I'm...I'm fine. It's just..." The words catch in my throat as I meet his piercing blue eyes.

"The mask," he says softly, understanding dawning. "Its pull is getting stronger."

I nod, unable to lie to him. "It wants me to go to him. To the Wolf King."

Vail steps closer, his presence both comforting and conflicting. "And what do you want, Lily?"

The question hangs in the air, heavy with unspoken emotions. I close my eyes, trying to sort through the tempest of feelings within me. "I want..." My voice falters. "I want to be free. But I don't know if that means going to the Wolf King or..."

"Or?" Vail prompts, his voice barely above a whisper.

I open my eyes, meeting his gaze. "Or staying with you."

The admission hangs between us, charged with possibility. Vail's hand reaches out, hesitating just shy of touching my cheek. "Lily, I—"

A howl echoes through the cavern, breaking the moment. Vail's expression hardens, his curse visibly struggling against him. "We need to keep moving," he growls, voice strained.

As we press on, the mask's pull intensifies, a constant war within me. Each step is a battle between duty and desire, between the unknown future with the Wolf King and the growing connection I feel with Vail. The red cloak pulses with power, a reminder of my heritage and the strength within me.

"Tell me about your life before," I say suddenly, desperate for distraction. "Before the curse."

Vail's steps falter for a moment. "It was...a lifetime ago. I was a different man then."

"Tell me," I insist, needing to hear his voice, to keep me from succumbing to the pull of the mask.

He sighs, a sound filled with centuries of regret. "I was a knight, sworn to protect the innocent. I believed in honor, in justice. But one mistake, one moment of weakness, and the Wolf King ensnared me."

The pain in his voice makes my heart ache. Without thinking, I reach out and take his hand. "You're still that man, Vail. I've seen it."

He looks at our joined hands, a mix of longing and fear in his eyes. "Am I? Or am I just the monster he made me?"

Before I can respond, a gust of icy wind sweeps through the cavern. The mask on my face grows cold, its whispers turning to shouts. Ahead, the lair of the Wolf King pulses with dark energy.

"We're here," Vail says grimly.

I squeeze his hand, torn between the pull of the

mask and the warmth of his touch. "Whatever happens, Vail, I—"

A deafening roar cuts me off, and the cavern begins to shake. The final test awaits, and I'm no longer sure which path I'll choose when the moment comes.

Six

The roar had to have come from the Wolf King, though I can't see him.

I step into the heart of the Wolf King's domain, my breath catching in my throat. The air here is thick with magic, heavy and oppressive, like a storm about to break. Shadows dance at the corners of my vision, teasing and taunting. Beside me, Vail's presence is a comforting warmth in this realm of cold malevolence.

"Grandmother," I whisper, my voice trembling as I spot her prone form on a stone altar. She looks so peaceful, as if merely asleep, but I know better. The enchantment holding her captive pulses with an eerie, sickly green light.

Vail's hand brushes against mine, a fleeting touch

that sends a shiver down my spine. "Be careful, Lily," he murmurs, his blue eyes scanning the shadows. "The Wolf King is near."

As if summoned by Vail's words, a figure materializes from the darkness. Tall and imposing, clothed in robes of midnight and silver, the Wolf King's mask gleams in the dim light. It looks exactly like the one Vail was wearing the day I first met him. My heart pounds against my ribs, a caged bird desperate for freedom.

"Welcome, little Red," the Wolf King purrs, his voice like honey laced with poison. "I've been expecting you."

I swallow hard, forcing my voice to remain steady. "Release my grandmother. Now."

A low chuckle reverberates through the chamber. "Oh, but where's the fun in that?" The Wolf King stalks closer, and I fight the urge to retreat. "I have a proposition for you, my dear."

My fingers curl into fists at my sides. "I'm not interested in any deals with you."

"Aren't you?" He cocks his head, the mask's empty eyes boring into me. "What if I told you I could free your grandmother? All it would take is one simple act."

Suspicion coils in my gut. "What act?"

The Wolf King reaches out, his fingers trailing along the edge of his mask. "Wear my mask. Join me as my queen. Free me from this prison, and I'll release your grandmother from hers."

I recoil, disgust and temptation warring within me. I rip the mask from my face and throw it at his feet. "Never," I spit.

"Think carefully, little Red," the Wolf King croons. "Power beyond your wildest dreams could be yours. All the mysteries of the magical realms, laid bare at your feet. Or..." He gestures towards my grandmother. "You could lose her forever."

I glance at Vail, hoping for guidance, but his face is a mask of stone. The weight of the choice settles on my shoulders, heavy as the world itself. My grandmother or my soul? How can I possibly decide?

Vail's voice cuts through my inner turmoil, low and dangerous. "Step away from her, Wolf King."

I turn to see Vail, his hand on the hilt of his sword, blue eyes blazing with a fury I've never witnessed before. The air around him crackles with tension, and I can almost see the battle between man and beast raging within him.

The Wolf King's laughter echoes through the chamber, a sound that sends shivers down my spine.

"Ah, my faithful knight. Have you forgotten your place?"

Vail draws his sword, the metal singing as it leaves its sheath. "My place is wherever I choose it to be."

He lunges forward, blade arcing through the air. For a moment, hope flares in my chest. But then the Wolf King raises a clawed hand, and Vail stumbles mid-strike, a pained growl tearing from his throat.

"Vail!" I cry out, reaching for him instinctively.

He turns to me, agony etched across his features. "Lily, don't—" His words cut off as another spasm wracks his body. I watch in horror as fur begins to sprout across his skin, his form twisting and contorting.

"What are you doing to him?" I demand, whirling on the Wolf King.

He shrugs, an elegant motion that belies the cruelty in his eyes. "Simply reminding him of what he truly is."

Vail's armor clatters to the ground as his body shifts, elongating into the form of a massive black wolf. His blue eyes, now feral and wild, lock onto mine for a brief moment before he throws his head back in a mournful howl.

"Stop it!" I plead, torn between rushing to Vail's

side and staying vigilant against the Wolf King. "Change him back!"

"I'm afraid I can't do that, my dear," the Wolf King purrs. "But you can."

The mask in his hands seems to pulse with dark energy, calling to something deep within me. I try to look away, but my gaze is drawn back, mesmerized by its shadowy depths.

"Think of the power you'd wield," the Wolf King's voice echoes in my mind, smooth as silk and sharp as a blade. "You could save them both—your grandmother and your knight. All it takes is one small sacrifice."

I shake my head, trying to clear it of his insidious whispers. "I won't become like you," I grit out, even as doubt gnaws at my resolve.

"Are you so sure?" he asks, and I can hear the smirk in his voice. "The mask calls to you, doesn't it? It recognizes the darkness within you, the potential for greatness."

My heart races, torn between the allure of his promises and the horror of what accepting might mean. I look at my grandmother, peaceful in her enchanted sleep, then to Vail, now a wolf pacing restlessly, caught between two worlds.

"Power beyond imagination," the Wolf King

continues, his words a seductive caress against my mind. "The ability to reshape reality itself. All this could be yours, Lily. All you have to do is reach out and take it."

My hand trembles as I extend it, fingers hovering mere inches from the mask. The pull is almost irresistible now, a siren song of power and possibility. But as I stare into its empty eyes, I see not just my reflection, but the echoes of all those who came before—trapped, consumed, lost.

I curl my fingers into a fist, drawing my hand back. "No," I whisper, my voice gaining strength as I repeat, "No. I won't be your puppet."

The Wolf King's eyes narrow, his patience clearly wearing thin. "Then you condemn them both to their fates. Is that truly what you want, little Red?"

Tears sting my eyes as I look between Vail and my grandmother, the weight of my choice crushing down upon me. How can I possibly decide? How can I live with myself no matter what I choose?

I take a deep breath, steeling myself for what I'm about to do. The air around us crackles with tension, heavy with the weight of magic and consequences.

"Wait," I say, my voice barely above a whisper. The Wolf King's eyes gleam with interest, and I force myself to meet his gaze. "I...I have a proposition."

A slow, predatory smile spreads across his face. "Oh? Do tell, little Red."

I swallow hard, my throat suddenly dry. "I'll stay with you," I begin, watching as triumph flashes in his eyes. "But," I continue quickly, "Nothing more. I will not be your queen."

The Wolf King's laughter echoes through the chamber, a sound that sends chills down my spine. "You think you can bargain with me? How...delightful."

"Those are my terms," I insist, trying to keep the tremor from my voice. "Take it or leave it."

He studies me for a long moment, his gaze so intense I feel as though he's peering into my very soul. "Very well," he says at last. "But know this, Lily Rhodes—once you put on that mask, there's no going back."

My heart breaks at the thought of never seeing Gran again, of staying with the Wolf King and not Vail.

But at least they'll be safe.

I nod, my heart pounding so loudly I'm sure he can hear it. With shaking hands, I reach for the mask. The moment my fingers touch its surface, I feel a jolt of energy course through me.

"Remember," the Wolf King purrs, "power comes at a price."

Taking one last look at Vail, still in his wolf form, I close my eyes and press the mask to my face. The world explodes into darkness, and then...

Power. Raw, unbridled power floods through me, setting every nerve ending alight. It's intoxicating, terrifying, exhilarating. I gasp, overwhelmed by the sensation.

"Open your eyes, my queen," the Wolf King's voice whispers in my mind.

I want to correct him, that I'm not his queen, but he's tricked me.

I open my eyes, and the world has changed. Everything is sharper, more vibrant. I can see the threads of magic weaving through the air, can feel the pulse of the forest around us.

"Now," I say, my voice resonating with newfound strength, "free my grandmother and Vail."

As the words leave my lips, I feel the dark power within me stir, eager to be unleashed. And in that moment, I realize the true weight of the bargain I've struck.

SEVEN

The mask melds to my skin, its power surging through my veins like liquid fire. I gasp, overwhelmed by the raw strength coursing through me. The Wolf King's realm unfolds before my eyes, a shadowy landscape of twisted trees and mist-shrouded hollows. I can feel every root, every leaf, every creature within its boundaries.

"This...this is incredible," I whisper, my voice echoing with newfound authority. The trees seem to bow in response, their branches swaying in a nonexistent breeze.

But even as I revel in this intoxicating power, a small voice in the back of my mind screams in protest. This isn't me. This isn't who I am.

A low growl breaks through my thoughts. I turn to see a massive wolf, fur as dark as midnight, eyes a familiar piercing blue. *Vail.*

"Lily," he growls, his voice rough yet unmistakable. "You must fight this. The mask...it's consuming you."

I shake my head, trying to clear the fog that's settled over my thoughts. "Vail?"

"The curse," he replies, padding closer. "It's complete now. Lily, remember who you are."

His words stir something within me, a memory of warm sunlight filtering through antique shop windows, of my grandmother's gentle smile. But the mask's influence is strong, whispering promises of power and control.

"I can feel everything, Vail," I say, my voice trembling with barely contained energy. "The entire realm...it's mine to command. Do you know what that feels like?"

Vail's eyes, so human despite his lupine form, fill with sorrow. "I do, Lily. And I know the price that comes with it. Please, listen to me. Remember our connection. Remember your humanity."

I reach out, my fingers brushing against his fur. The touch sends a jolt through me, a reminder of stolen moments and unspoken feelings. For a brief instant, the mask's hold weakens.

"I...I don't know if I can fight this," I admit, my voice barely above a whisper. The trees around us seem to lean in, as if listening to our exchange. "It's so strong, Vail. So tempting."

Vail presses his muzzle against my hand. "You are stronger, Lily Rhodes. You've always been stronger than you know. Don't let the mask take that away from you."

I close my eyes, torn between the seductive pull of power and the warmth of Vail's presence. The forest holds its breath, waiting to see which path I'll choose.

The air shimmers, and suddenly, the Wolf King materializes before us. His presence is overwhelming, a palpable force that makes the very trees around us tremble. His eyes, molten gold and filled with ancient wisdom, lock onto mine.

"Lily Rhodes," he purrs, his voice like velvet over steel. "You've tasted true power. Imagine what we could accomplish together."

I feel Vail tense beside me, but my attention is captivated by the visions the Wolf King weaves. The magical realms of Stormwind unfold before my eyes, a tapestry of wonder and chaos.

"Look," the Wolf King urges, gesturing to the scenes playing out before us. "See how the balance has been disrupted. With your strength and my knowledge, we could restore harmony. We could rule, side by side."

My heart races. The mask pulses against my skin, whispering promises of greatness. "I... I could help people?" I ask, my voice small against the enormity of the offer.

The Wolf King's smile is both beautiful and terrifying. "You could save them all, my dear. Your power would be unmatched."

I take a step forward, entranced. The visions grow more vivid—I see myself, resplendent in power, shaping the very fabric of reality.

"Lily, no!" Vail's desperate howl cuts through my reverie. "He's lying!"

But the mask tightens its grip, flooding my veins with intoxicating strength. I can feel the Wolf King's approval, his dark satisfaction.

"Join me," he coaxes, extending a clawed hand. "Embrace your destiny."

I reach out, my fingers trembling. The forest holds its breath.

Then, like a ray of sunlight breaking through

storm clouds, I hear my grandmother's voice. A memory, clear as crystal: "I love you, my little Red."

It grounds me.

I gasp, my hand faltering. "No," I whisper, then louder, "No! This isn't what I want!"

The Wolf King's eyes narrow. "You cannot resist your true nature," he growls.

But I stand my ground, feeling the weight of my duty, of generations of Red Cloaks before me. "My nature," I say, my voice growing stronger, "is to protect, not to rule. And I won't let you or this mask change that."

I lock eyes with Vail, his wolf form trembling with barely contained energy. The connection between us pulses, a lifeline in this maelstrom of dark magic. I reach out, not with my hand, but with my mind, my heart, my very essence.

"Vail," I whisper, my voice barely audible above the howling wind. "I see you."

The Wolf King snarls, his façade of charm crumbling. "He is mine, girl. Bound by blood and curse."

But I ignore him, focusing solely on Vail. His blue eyes, still so human despite his lupine form, meet mine. In them, I see centuries of pain, of longing, of a noble spirit trapped in darkness.

"Remember who you were," I urge, taking a step closer. The air crackles with tension, and I can feel the mask's power surging, trying to overwhelm me. But I push back, channeling every ounce of my will into our connection. "You're more than his puppet, Vail. You're a knight, a protector."

Vail whimpers, his massive form shuddering. I can almost see the threads of the curse, black and oily, wrapping around him.

The Wolf King lunges forward, his claws extended. "Enough! I command you to obey!"

But his words lack their usual power. I feel it—a weakening, a fracture in his control. My heart races as I press on.

"Vail, take my hand," I say, extending my fingers towards him. "Break free. I believe in you."

Time seems to slow. I can hear my heartbeat, feel the pulse of magic in the air. The Wolf King roars in fury, but it sounds distant, muffled.

Vail's eyes never leave mine as he slowly, painfully, raises his paw. The moment we touch, it's like a thunderclap. Energy surges between us, pure and bright. I gasp as I feel the curse shatter, its hold on Vail dissolving like mist in sunlight.

The Wolf King staggers back, his face contorted in disbelief and rage. "Impossible!" he howls.

But I know it's true. I can feel Vail's humanity flooding back, his spirit breaking free. And with it, I sense the Wolf King's power diminishing, his hold on this realm weakening.

"It's over," I say, my voice ringing with newfound strength. "Your reign ends now."

Eight

The Wolf King's eyes gleam with malice as I step into the shadowy throne room, my heart pounding. Vail's presence beside me is a steadying force, his armor creaking softly with each measured step. The mask pulses against my skin, whispering dark promises.

"So, little Red has come to challenge me at last," the Wolf King sneers, his voice like gravel. "Tell me, child, do you truly believe you can defeat me?"

I swallow hard, feeling the mask's power coursing through me. It would be so easy to strike him down, to claim his throne and reshape this realm as I see fit. My fingers twitch, longing to unleash that raw energy.

"I've come to end your reign of terror," I say,

proud that my voice doesn't waver. "Your darkness has poisoned these lands for too long."

The Wolf King laughs, a harsh sound that echoes off the stone walls. "And what will you do, little one? Destroy me? Take my place?"

I hesitate, the weight of the decision crushing down on me. The mask thrums insistently, urging me to act. But a seed of doubt takes root in my mind.

"Lily," Vail murmurs, his voice low and urgent. "Remember why we're here. Trust your instincts."

I look up at him, seeing centuries of pain etched in the lines of his face. How many others have suffered under the Wolf King's rule? And yet...

The throne room seems to darken, shadows writhing at the edges of my vision. The air grows thick with tension as I stand frozen, caught between duty and doubt.

"You hesitate," the Wolf King growls, leaning forward on his throne. "Perhaps you're not as strong as you thought."

His words sting, but they also clear my mind. I straighten my shoulders, meeting his gaze.

"Strength isn't about destruction," I say, surprised by the conviction in my own voice. "It's about making the right choice, even when it's difficult."

The mask pulses angrily against my skin, but I ignore its siren song.

As I stand there, poised on the knife's edge of decision, I can feel the weight of both realms pressing down upon me. The musty scent of ancient stone mingles with the metallic tang of Vail's armor and the acrid smell of the Wolf King's dark magic. Every sense is heightened, every moment stretching into eternity as I grapple with the enormity of my choice.

The Wolf King's eyes gleam with malevolent intelligence as he leans forward, his voice a seductive purr. "Why fight it, Lily? The power coursing through you, it's intoxicating, isn't it? You could reshape both realms to your will. No more hiding in the shadows, no more fear."

His words slither into my mind, tempting and treacherous. I feel the mask's energy pulsing in sync with my quickening heartbeat. For a moment, I see flashes of a world remade in my image—beautiful, but terrible.

"Don't listen to him," Vail's low voice cuts through my reverie. I turn to meet his piercing blue gaze, seeing centuries of sorrow and wisdom there. "Trust your heart, Lily. It's what brought you this far."

I swallow hard, torn between the seductive

promise of absolute power and the steady warmth of Vail's faith in me. "But what if I'm not strong enough?" I whisper, voicing my deepest fear.

Vail's hand finds mine, his touch grounding me. "You are. I've seen your compassion, your resilience. That's true strength."

The Wolf King snarls, shadows whirling around him. "Enough! Choose, girl. Take my place or fall to ruin!"

In that moment, clarity washes over me like a cool spring rain. I raise my hands, feeling the mask's power surge through me. But instead of striking out, I focus inward, channeling that energy into a different purpose.

"I choose neither," I declare, my voice ringing with newfound certainty. "I choose balance."

With every ounce of will I possess, I direct the mask's power not to destroy, but to bind. Tendrils of light and shadow intertwine, weaving a intricate cage around the Wolf King. He howls in fury, but I stand firm, sweat beading on my brow as I complete the spell.

"You will remain," I tell him, my voice barely above a whisper, "but your influence will be contained. The realms will find their own balance."

As the last threads of magic settle into place, I

feel the curse lifting, its weight dissipating like morning mist. I turn to Vail, seeing a spark of hope in his eyes for the first time.

"It's done," I breathe, exhaustion and elation warring within me. "We've broken the curse without destroying everything."

The ground beneath my feet trembles, and a deafening crack echoes through the air. I stumble, my heart racing as I realize the implications of what we've done.

"Lily!" Vail's voice cuts through the chaos. "The realm is collapsing. We need to move, now!"

I nod, my eyes scanning the crumbling landscape. Trees groan and splinter, their roots tearing free from the disintegrating earth. The sky above us swirls with ominous, dark clouds, flashes of otherworldly lightning illuminating the destruction.

"Grandmother," I gasp, remembering why I came here in the first place.

Vail grabs my hand, his touch sending a jolt of electricity through me even in this dire moment. "This way," he says, pulling me towards where my grandmother is now laying on the ground.

"Grandma!" I cry out, rushing forward.

She looks up, her eyes wide with disbelief. "Lily? Is it really you?"

I help her to her feet, noticing how frail she seems. "It's me, Grandma. We're getting you out of here."

Vail's voice cuts through our reunion. "We need to go. The barrier between worlds is weakening."

As if to emphasize his point, a massive fissure opens up in the ground behind us, swallowing trees and earth alike. The air crackles with wild magic, making my skin prickle.

"How do we get back?" I ask, supporting my grandmother as we stumble out of her prison.

Vail's face is grim. "The same way we came in. But it won't be easy. The forest is sealing itself away."

We start running, dodging falling debris and leaping over newly formed chasms. The once-lush forest is now a maze of destruction, barely recognizable. I can feel the magic of this realm slipping away, like water through cupped hands.

"There!" Vail shouts, pointing to a shimmering distortion in the air ahead of us. "That's our way out!"

As we sprint towards our escape, I can't help but look back. The Wolf King's realm, for all its darkness and danger, had also been a place of wonder and magic. A part of me aches to see it disappear.

"Lily, focus!" Vail's voice snaps me back to the

present. We're almost at the portal, but it's shrinking rapidly.

With one last burst of speed, we plunge through the portal, the magical forest vanishing behind us in a blinding flash of light.

Nine

The mask stares at me from my dresser, its empty eyes a void that seems to pull at my very soul. I shiver, wrapping my arms around myself as I gaze out the window of my tiny apartment. Stormwind bustles below, oblivious to the magic that lurks in its shadows.

"You don't have to keep it, you know," Vail's deep voice rumbles from behind me.

I turn to face him, drinking in the sight of him lounging on my secondhand couch. His dark hair falls across his forehead, softening the sharp angles of his face. He looks...almost human now.

"I can't just throw it away," I murmur, my fingers tracing the cool surface of the mask. "It's a part of me now."

Vail's piercing blue eyes meet mine. "Is it? Or are you just afraid to let it go?"

His words strike a chord deep within me. Am I holding onto the mask out of duty, or fear? The power it once held courses through my veins like a drug, tempting and terrifying all at once.

"I don't know who I am without it anymore," I confess, my voice barely above a whisper.

Vail rises from the couch, his movements fluid and graceful. He crosses the room to stand before me, close enough that I can feel the heat radiating from his body.

"You're Lily Rhodes," he says softly, his hand cupping my cheek. "Brave, compassionate, and stronger than you know."

I lean into his touch, closing my eyes against the sudden sting of tears. "And who are you now, Vail? Without the curse, without the Wolf King?"

His hand falls away, and I open my eyes to see a shadow pass over his face. "I'm... not sure," he admits. "The wolves still call to me, but it's different now. Gentler."

I watch as he paces the small confines of my apartment, his broad shoulders hunched with the weight of uncertainty. "Do you regret it?" I ask, fear coiling in my stomach. "Breaking free?"

Vail stops, turning to face me with an intensity that steals my breath. "Never," he growls. "But this world...your world...it's so different from what I've known. The noise, the smells, the sheer number of people...it's overwhelming."

I cross to him, driven by an impulse I can't quite name. My hand finds his, our fingers intertwining. "We'll figure it out together," I promise, even as doubt gnaws at my insides. "One day at a time."

Vail's thumb traces slow circles on the back of my hand, sending shivers up my arm. "And what of your life here, Lily? Your grandmother's shop, your friends...can you truly go back to that after everything you've seen?"

The question hangs in the air between us, heavy with implications. I think of the antique shop, of the dusty shelves filled with artifacts whose true nature I now understand. I think of my friends, laughing over coffee, blissfully unaware of the magic that threads through our city.

"I don't know," I admit, my voice barely audible over the hum of traffic outside. "But I have to try."

The scent of lavender and chamomile wafts through the air as I push open the door to my grandmother's room. Sunlight streams through the lace curtains, casting intricate patterns on the patchwork quilt covering her frail form. My heart skips a beat as I see her sitting up, her silver hair neatly braided, a spark of life returned to her eyes.

"Lily, my dear," she says, her voice stronger than I've heard in weeks. "Come, sit with me. We have much to discuss."

I perch on the edge of the bed, my fingers tracing the familiar patterns of the quilt. "Grandma, you're looking so much better. I was worried that—"

She waves away my concern with a brittle hand. "Hush now. There are things you need to know, truths I should have shared long ago."

A chill runs down my spine despite the warmth of the room. "What do you mean?"

Grandmother's eyes, the same deep green as my own, lock onto mine. "I was a Red Cloak, Lily. Just like you. And I've always known this day would come."

The world tilts on its axis. "You...you knew? All this time?"

She nods, a sad smile playing on her lips. "Our lineage stretches back centuries, intertwined with the very fabric of magic itself. The shop, the artifacts...they were never just antiques. They were our legacy, our responsibility."

I struggle to process this revelation. "But why didn't you tell me? Why let me stumble into all of this blind?"

"Oh, my dear," she sighs, reaching for my hand. Her touch is cool, grounding. "Some truths can't be told; they must be lived. You had to discover your strength on your own."

Tears prick at the corners of my eyes. "I was so scared, Grandma. I still am. The power I felt when I wore the mask... it was intoxicating. Terrifying."

Her grip on my hand tightens. "That's the final secret, Lily. The mask, the cloak...they're just conduits. The true power has always been within you. In your heart, your choices."

I close my eyes, remembering the rush of energy, the temptation. "How do I control it? How do I know I won't...lose myself?"

"By remembering who you are," she says softly. "By surrounding yourself with those who see your light, even in the darkest moments."

Vail's face flashes in my mind, his blue eyes filled with a mix of awe and understanding. I open my mouth to ask about him, about us, but a knock at the door interrupts.

"Come in," my grandmother calls, a knowing glint in her eye.

Vail steps into the room, his presence filling the space. Our eyes meet, and I feel that familiar pull, the connection that defies explanation.

"I hope I'm not interrupting," he says, his deep voice sending a shiver down my spine.

"Not at all," my grandmother replies. "In fact, your timing is perfect. Lily needs all the support she can get as she steps into her new role."

I look between them, feeling the weight of destiny settling on my shoulders. "And what exactly is that role?"

My grandmother's smile is enigmatic. "That, my dear, is for you to decide. The path of a Red Cloak is never straight, but it is always meaningful."

I stand, my legs shaky but my resolve strengthening. Vail's hand slides from my shoulder, his fingers briefly intertwining with mine. The touch sends a spark through me, igniting something primal and urgent.

"Can we talk?" I ask him, my voice barely above a whisper.

He nods, those piercing blue eyes never leaving

mine. We step out into the hallway, the air between us charged with unspoken words. I lead him to my room, closing the door behind us with a soft click.

"Lily," he begins, his voice thick with emotion. "I need you to know something."

I turn to face him, my heart pounding. "What is it?"

He takes a deep breath, his broad chest rising and falling. "Your strength...it's not from the mask. It never was. It's here." He places his hand gently over my heart, and I feel it skip a beat.

"But the power I felt..." I trail off, remembering the intoxicating rush.

"Was always within you," he finishes. "The mask merely awakened what was already there."

I look up at him, searching his face. "How can you be so sure?"

His lips quirk into a small smile. "Because I've watched you grow into the remarkable woman you are today. I've seen your courage, your compassion, your unwavering spirit."

My breath catches in my throat. "You've...watched me?"

Vail's eyes soften, a vulnerability I've never seen before shining through. "I've been your guardian,

Lily. From the shadows, I've watched over you all your life."

"Why?" I whisper, though deep down, I already know the answer.

He cups my face in his hands, his touch infinitely gentle. "Because I love you. I have for longer than I can remember."

The confession hangs in the air between us, electric and raw. I reach up, tracing the line of his jaw with my fingertips. "Vail, I-"

His lips crash into mine, cutting off my words. The kiss is desperate, hungry, years of longing poured into a single moment. I melt into him, my body molding against his as if we were two pieces of a long-lost puzzle.

His hands slide down my back, pulling me closer as our kiss deepens. I tangle my fingers in his hair, savoring the silky strands between my fingertips. A low growl rumbles in his chest as he walks me backward until my legs hit the edge of the bed.

We tumble onto the mattress, a tangle of limbs and gasping breaths. Vail's weight presses me into the quilt, deliciously solid and real. His lips trail fire down my neck, teeth grazing my collarbone. I arch into him, craving more, craving everything.

"Lily," he rasps against my skin. "Are you sure?"

In answer, I pull his mouth back to mine, pouring every ounce of certainty into the kiss. There is no hesitation, no doubt—only the overwhelming need to be as close to him as possible.

Our clothes fall away, piece by piece, until there is nothing left between us but heat and desire. Vail's hands map every curve and hollow of my body, leaving trails of goosebumps in their wake. I explore the hard planes of his chest, the corded muscles of his arms, committing every inch of him to memory.

When he finally sinks into me, I cry out, my nails digging into his shoulders. He stills, allowing me to adjust to the exquisite stretch and fullness. And then he begins to move, long, deep strokes that send pleasure spiraling through every nerve ending.

I meet him thrust for thrust, our bodies moving in a primal rhythm as old as time itself. The world narrows to this room, this bed, this man. Nothing else exists but the slide of skin against skin, the mingling of breath and heartbeats.

Vail's thrusts grow harder, faster, driving me towards the edge. I cling to him, my anchor in the storm of sensation. When I shatter, he swallows my cries with his mouth, holding me as I come apart in his arms.

With a final, shuddering groan, he finds his own

release, spilling deep inside me. We lay tangled together, sweat cooling on our skin, hearts gradually slowing. In this moment, the ghosts of our pasts, the uncertainties of our future, fade away. There is only the two of us, bound by something far deeper than magic or destiny.

"I love you," I murmur into the crook of his neck. "I think I have for a long time."

Vail's arms tighten around me. "And I will love you, Lily Rhodes, for as long as I draw breath."

As I drift towards sleep, safe in the circle of his embrace, I know that whatever challenges lie ahead, we will face them together. The Red Cloak and the Cursed Knight, united at last. And for the first time since donning the mask, I feel a flicker of hope.

TEN

I watch in awe as the gnarled trees straighten, their twisted branches unfurling like awakening limbs. The oppressive mist that has cloaked the forest for so long dissipates, revealing dappled sunlight dancing on verdant leaves. The air, once thick with the acrid scent of dark magic, now carries the sweet perfume of wildflowers and fresh earth.

"It's beautiful," I breathe, my voice barely above a whisper.

Beside me, Vail shifts. "Appearances can be deceiving, Lily. The danger may have receded, but it is not gone entirely."

His words send a shiver down my spine, despite

the warmth of the sun on my skin. I turn to face him, searching those piercing blue eyes for answers. "You can still sense it?"

A muscle twitches in his jaw. "As can you, I suspect. The forest may look peaceful, but there's an undercurrent of...something. A lingering trace of what once was."

I nod, feeling the truth of his words resonate within me. The forest looks normal, yet there's a vibration in the air, a tension that sets my nerves on edge. My fingers twitch, longing for the reassuring weight of my grandmother's red cloak.

"We should check on the Wolf King's domain," I say, the words tasting bitter on my tongue. "Make sure nothing remains that could pose a threat."

Vail's gaze softens slightly. "Are you certain you're ready for that?"

I swallow hard, memories of our last encounter with the Wolf King flashing through my mind. The clash of steel, the searing pain of magic, the heart-wrenching moment when I thought I'd lost Vail forever. My hand unconsciously reaches for his, our fingers intertwining.

"I have to be," I reply, forcing steel into my voice. "As long as that mask exists, there's a chance someone could use its power again. We need to make sure it's locked away for good."

Vail nods, a flicker of pride crossing his features. Without another word, we set off deeper into the forest. As we walk, I can't shake the feeling that unseen eyes are watching our every move. The leaves whisper secrets as we pass, and shadows seem to dance just beyond the corner of my vision.

We reach the crumbling ruins of the Wolf King's fortress, its once-imposing walls now reduced to little more than rubble. I pause at the entrance, my heart racing. Vail's hand on my shoulder steadies me.

"You don't have to do this alone," he murmurs.

I take a deep breath, drawing strength from his presence. "I know. But I need to be the one to put it away. To make sure it can never hurt anyone again."

Steeling myself, I step into the ruins. The mask lies where we left it, its blank eyes seeming to follow our movements. I approach cautiously, remembering all too well the seductive whisper of its power.

"Over here," Vail calls, gesturing to a hidden alcove. "This should suffice as a vault."

I nod, carefully lifting the mask. Its weight feels impossibly heavy in my hands, a burden of responsibility I never asked for but can't ignore. As I place it in the alcove, I whisper a prayer to whatever forces might be listening.

"Let this be the end of it," I plead softly. "Let the magic sleep."

Vail steps forward, his hands moving in an intricate pattern as he mutters an incantation. The air shimmers, and the alcove seems to fade from view, becoming just another unremarkable part of the crumbling wall.

As we turn to leave, I can't shake the feeling that this is far from over. The forest may be healing, the immediate threat may have passed, but deep in my bones, I know my role as protector is only beginning. The thought both terrifies and exhilarates me, a destiny I never wanted but can no longer deny.

***

The autumn leaves crunch beneath my feet as I make my way to the clearing where the Red Cloaks gather. My heart pounds in my chest, a mix of anticipation and dread coursing through my veins. Grandmother stands at the center, her silver hair gleaming in the fading sunlight, her red cloak billowing gently in the breeze.

"Lily," she calls, her voice carrying a weight I've never heard before. "Come forward, child."

I approach, acutely aware of the eyes of every Red Cloak upon me. The air is thick with expectation, and I can almost taste the magic that still lingers in this place, a reminder of the two worlds we straddle.

"It's time," Grandmother says, her green eyes—so like my own—searching my face. "The mantle of leadership must pass to you."

I swallow hard, my voice barely a whisper. "But Grandmother, I'm not ready. I still have so much to learn."

She smiles, a hint of sadness in her expression. "None of us are ever truly ready, Lily. But you have proven yourself time and again. You understand the delicate balance between our world and theirs better than anyone."

As she unfastens her cloak, I can't help but think of all I'll be giving up. "What about my life in Stormwind? The antique shop? My friends?"

"Your duty doesn't mean abandoning your life," Grandmother assures me, draping the cloak around my shoulders. Its weight settles on me, both comforting and suffocating. "It means living between both worlds, as you always have. Only now, you'll be their guardian."

I close my eyes, feeling the soft fabric against my skin, imagining all the generations of women who wore it before me. When I open them again, I see Vail at the edge of the clearing, his blue eyes fixed on me with an intensity that makes my breath catch.

"I accept," I say, my voice stronger now. "I will watch over both worlds, as the Red Cloaks have always done."

A cheer goes up from the gathered crowd, but all I can focus on is Vail's slight nod of approval. As the ceremony concludes, he makes his way to my side, his presence a comforting constant in this sea of change.

"How does it feel?" he asks, his voice low and intimate.

I shrug, a wry smile tugging at my lips. "Heavy. Terrifying. Exhilarating."

Vail's hand finds mine, his touch sending a familiar thrill through me. "You won't face it alone," he says. "I'll always be by your side, Lily."

My heart soars at his words.

He wraps an arm around me and pulls me close, and I melt against him.

He'll always be my knight in shining armor.

As we stand there, the last rays of sunlight casting long shadows across the clearing, I can't help but feel a mix of hope and trepidation. The weight of my new role presses down on me, but with Vail by my side, I know we can face whatever challenges lie ahead.

Don't miss the rest of the Spicy Romantasy series! Go to www.authorkenzieskye.com to find out where to get the rest of the series and to get a free book!